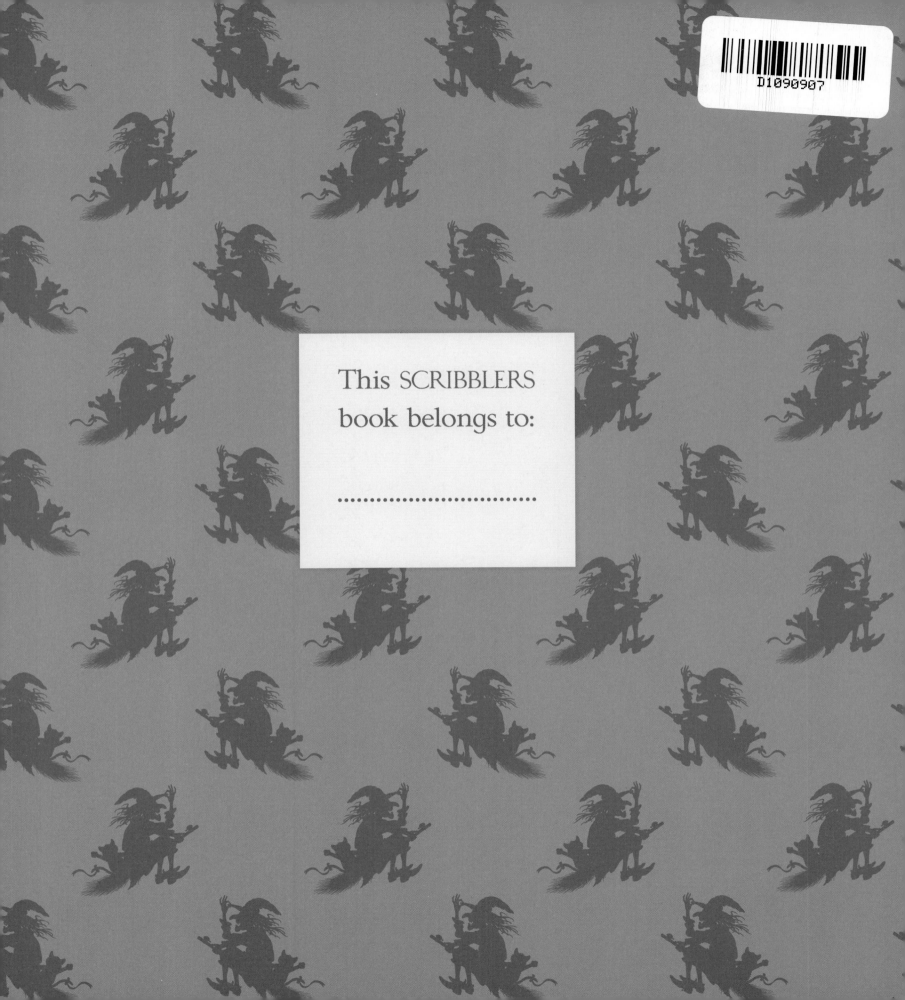

This SCRIBBLERS
book belongs to:

....

Trixie
The Witch's Cat

Nick Butterworth

SCRIBBLERS
a SALARIYA *imprint*

Trixie, the witch's cat, was a happy cat. Most of the time. There was only one thing that could make Trixie really unhappy and, luckily, it was something Trixie didn't think about.

Most of the time.

But then, sometimes, Trixie just couldn't help it.

Then, Trixie the happy cat, became Trixie, the very-unhappy-indeed cat.

She would go into a bad mood, as if a dark thundercloud had settled over her head.

She threw things, kicked things and shouted all sorts of things.

'I hate this horrible, ugly paw!' Trixie would shout. And if anyone ever dared to ask why, Trixie would only say, 'Because...it's ugly and it's horrible!'

Trixie's 'horrible, ugly paw' was really a very nice paw. It was the right size and shape and the claws worked properly. It was beautifully fluffy and it was...white.

And that was the problem. Trixie knew for certain that witches' cats did not have white paws, because...because... well, they just didn't.

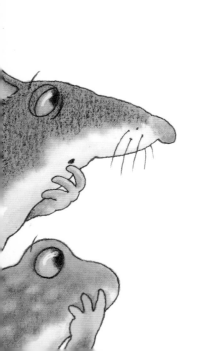

Trixie tried to keep her white paw hidden, especially when the other witch's cats were about. It was very inconvenient and it wasn't the answer.

Hi Trixie! Want to come and play?

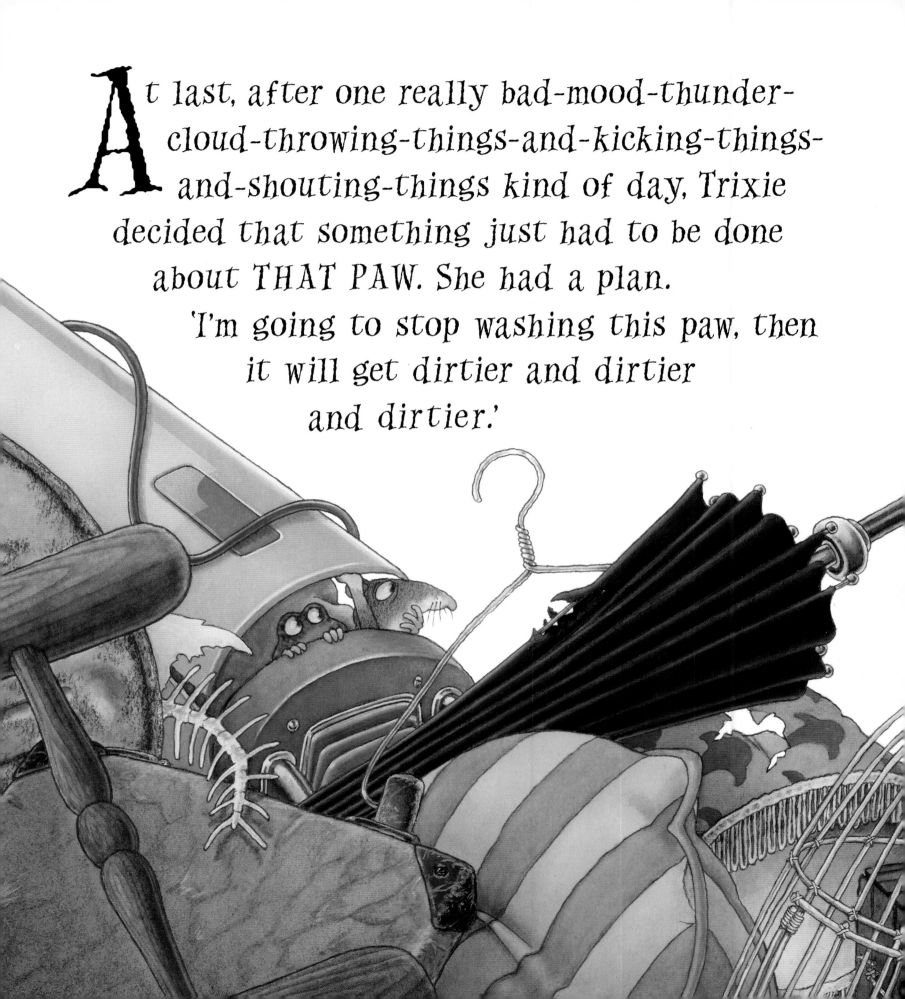

At last, after one really bad-mood-thunder-cloud-throwing-things-and-kicking-things-and-shouting-things kind of day, Trixie decided that something just had to be done about THAT PAW. She had a plan.

'I'm going to stop washing this paw, then it will get dirtier and dirtier and dirtier.'

Trixie thought, if she left it long enough, it would go nice and black, like her other paws. 'I'm not going to wash it for a hundred years,' she said.

At first, Trixie was pleased with her plan. She stopped washing her paw and it did get dirtier and dirtier.

But it didn't go black. And after only three weeks of her one hundred years, Trixie's paw began to smell. Badly. REALLY badly.

Trixie had an idea that she would paint her paw black. It was NOT a good idea.

Suddenly, Trixie had another idea.
A brilliant idea, she thought.
'Of course!' she said. 'I'm a
witch's cat. I'll use MAGIC
to turn my paw black!'

irst, Trixie borrowed the witch's wand and her book of spells. Then she got busy with a very important piece of magic...

ONE PINCH OF BLACK PEPPER,
BLACK HAIR FROM CAT'S FOOT.
TWO BLACKBIRD FEATHERS,
THREE BUCKETS OF SOOT.
BLACK TREACLE,
BLACKBERRIES,
THIRTEEN TIMES TWO.
BUBBLE AND BOIL IN
A BLACK,
WITCHY
BREW!

Suddenly...

Trixie was amazed to find that she had not been hurt. She could easily comb her hair over a patch on top of her head where she had lost some fur. But as she looked into the mirror, Trixie was even more amazed.

She was delighted to see that her white paw was black! Her magic had worked! Hooray! At last, Trixie was a proper, black, witch's cat. Just like all the others.

But, oh dear. Now, it was impossible to tell which one of the witch's cats was Trixie and which one wasn't.

No one could say which witch's cat was which. Without her white paw, even Trixie wondered which one she was.

It was then that Trixie began
to miss her old white paw.
Her nice white paw.
Her lovely white paw.
She really did. And now
it was gone. Forever.

Trixie started
to cry.

As Trixie wiped away a tear with her new black paw, something very strange happened. The black began to fade. First, to dark grey...

...snowy white! What was going on? Could it be that Trixie's magic was not very strong? Or was there stronger magic in Trixie's tears?

...then to light grey,
then lighter and lighter,
until Trixie's paw was...

Trixie had no idea.
She only knew that her white paw,
which was just the right size and shape,
her paw with its properly working claws,
her perfectly beautiful, fluffy, WHITE paw,
was back where it belonged.

From that day, Trixie never again went into
a bad mood or threw things, or kicked things,
or shouted things. Well, hardly ever.
And never EVER about...
that paw.

Trixie was happy to be
just the way she was.

For
Thomas,
eleven
years
on
and
definitely
someone
to
look
up
to.

With heaps of love
from Grandpa x

This edition published in MMXXI
by Scribblers, an imprint of
The Salariya Book Company Ltd
25 Marlborough Place,
Brighton BN1 1UB
www.salariya.com

SALARIYA
SCRIBO BOOK HOUSE SCRIBBLERS

First published in Great Britain in MMIX by Puffin
© The Salariya Book Company Ltd MMXXII
Text and illustrations © Nick Butterworth MMXXII

HB ISBN-13: 978-1-913971-15-1

1 3 5 7 9 8 6 4 2

A CIP catalogue record for this book is
available from the British Library.

Printed and bound in China.

Printed on paper from sustainable sources.

Visit
www.salariya.com
for our online catalogue and
free fun stuff.